IT'S WRITTEN IN THE

Let Your Feminine Star Joyfully Shine

VIKTORIA I. PIERCE

IT'S WRITTEN IN THE STARS
Let Your Feminine Star Joyfully Shine

Book Design by
Transcendent Publishing
www.transcendentpublishing.com

ISBN: 979-8-9885147-6-3

Printed in the United States of America.

"You are always free to change your mind and choose
a different future, or a different past."
–Richard Bach, *Illusions: The Adventures
of a Reluctant Messiah*

CONTENTS

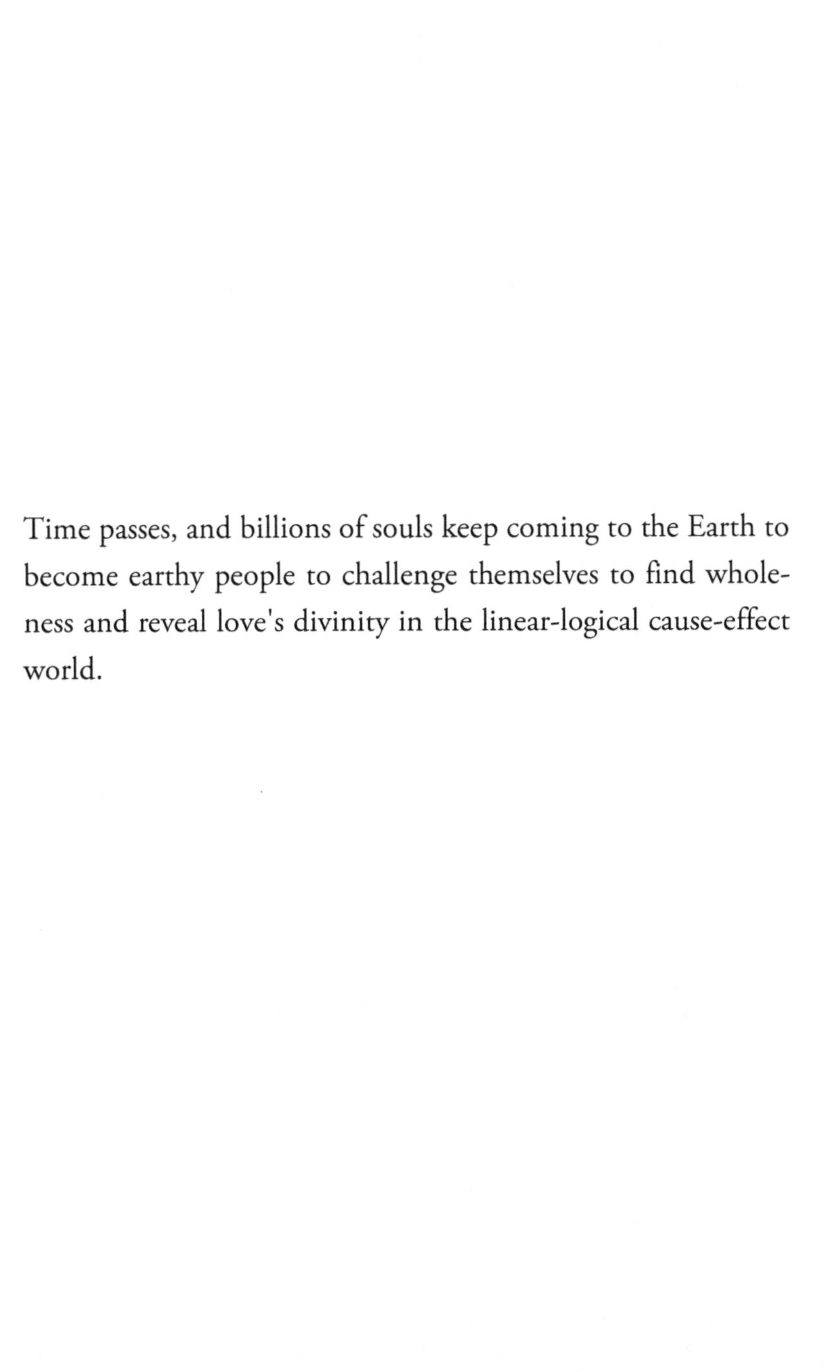

Time passes, and billions of souls keep coming to the Earth to become earthy people to challenge themselves to find wholeness and reveal love's divinity in the linear-logical cause-effect world.

INTRODUCTION

It was a beautiful sunny day in Bad Reichenhall, Germany. The first part of the Hellinger Camp seminar had just ended, and I couldn't think of a better way to spend my two-hour break than walking along the park's paths.

As I stepped between colorful, fragrant flower beds, enjoying the view of a giant fountain with snow-covered hills in the background, I reflected on all I'd just learned. That morning, philosopher Bert Hellinger had demonstrated how his discoveries of the Orders of Love and Conscience influence human relationships and the circumstances of one's daily life.

It was amazing to be immersed in the invisible dimensions of life where there is no distinction between right and wrong, between you and me. After many hours of meditation and heart-touching constellations, my mind was tranquil and I was experiencing deep inner peace.

I stopped to look at the noisy fountain throwing water streams, and the beams of sunlight penetrating the rustling, heart-shaped leaves of huge lindens. Suddenly, I saw on the inner screen of my mind many generations of crying women. There were thousands of them, grieving the husbands and children they had lost to wars and other cataclysms. Their pain resonated within me. It resonated with the pain I had inherited from the generations of women in my family who survived two world wars, the October Revolution, Stalin's repressions, and the forced starvations by the Soviet government in 1918 and 1933. They had suffered terrible losses. I feel their pain, and I take all of them into my heart with love.

I am grieving and crying with everyone who mourns the loss.

I feel scared with everyone who is frightened.

I'm in a fury together with everyone who is in rage.

I'm reliant on the best outcome with everyone who is hoping.

I feel fondness with everyone who is in love.

I feel frustrated and anxious with everyone who is distressed.

I'm lost with everyone who is hopeless.

I'm joyful with everyone blissful.

My heartbeats are aligned with the heartbeats of all humankind because I am a part of them. I'm not better, nor am I worse, than anybody else. Each of us has a unique place in the web of life and serves life in a way we were called to minister.

What I realized is that in peacetime or wartime, a woman, as a keeper of the hearth, as a mother and wife, bears the burden of responsibility in the name of love and the continuation of life. At the same time, her soul is looking for ways in which to bring about self-realization. I walked back into the seminar with new eyes, eager to know more about myself, the people around me, and the invisible forces that govern our lives.

Most of us don't see those invisible forces through which we are interconnected. We do not look at people around us as vessels for delivering messages from the Universe. Instead, we stand as billions of separate "I's" (isolated islands) against the crashing waves of challenges without a clear understanding of what to do and where to go. Our fear of being rejected for making a wrong decision tears our hearts and minds apart, creating painful feelings of loneliness.

This book is about women and their life choices, the endless internal conflict, and the search for love. It's about duality and integrity, and the invisible world of energy connections that can manifest through Family Constellations.

While navigating these pages, you will explore how duality creates drama, and how shifting from divisive judgment to unifying acceptance and reconciliation expands the space for new opportunities to unfold. Allow yourself to submerge, as I did, in the world of imaginative thinking where everything is possible.

My hope is that in reading this story, you will be enveloped in the feeling of love and relaxation that is your birthright.

PROLOGUE

Once upon a time, a child was born. Her parents called her Alice. The child was perfect and innocent in her wholeness. All planets and stars from near and far rejoiced and greeted this newborn keeper of life. In their cosmic dance, they formed a unique constellation to mark that precious moment of Alice's arrival on a universal calendar of events. The celestial beings sent divine blessings and numerous gifts to make her life journey meaningful and joyful.

From Mercury, there was a gift of creative expression, including intellect and memory; Mars delivered a burst of the active masculine energies of courage, passion, and confidence; Venus offered a wave of feminine power that included beauty, grace, and appreciation for the material things; and from Jupiter, there was luck, wealth, wisdom and spirituality. Saturn allowed the child to balance good and evil and follow discipline. Intuition, compassion, inspiration, and divinity arrived from Neptune. Pluto sent the energy of transformation, rebirth, and the ability to live her truth. Sun gave the child vitality and immunity, and Uranus guaranteed Alice's uniqueness. Earth embodied and grounded the energetic components of the gifts the child received from these various sources.

The divine gifts were filled with unconditional universal love and wrapped in eternal cosmic consciousness. The package arrived with a note engraved by a sunlight beam on a snowy white cloud that soon disappeared in the vast blue sky. If someone had only paid careful attention to the moment, they could have read the message:

Dear Soul,

Welcome to the planet Earth. It is beautiful, and the perfect place to explore and master your qualities within a space of duality. We have provided you with all the tools and support you need, and we will accompany you and be available for you on your journey. However, it is for you to decide whether you hear our advice and accept our help, which we will provide through other living creatures and events.

Please remember that everything has its opposite side in the world of duality; therefore, each gift we send to you can be used for good or for bad. Again, the choice is yours.

Very soon, your mind will divide everything into positive right and negative wrong; masculine and feminine; just and unjust. Your parents, teachers, and environment will take care of that to ensure you do not remember who you really are. Eventually, you will perceive yourself as broken into millions of tiny pieces which are in constant conflict with each other.

Your goal is to collect yourself while walking on a razor's edge. Much is predetermined, but nothing is fixed. Enjoy your journey. You cannot fail. Any experience you gain has great value as it enriches your qualities.

You are love. You are loved. Stay in Love.

CHAPTER ONE

A fresh summer breeze blew in through the open window and slightly parted the white tulle curtains. The tender light of the moon slipped into the room and illuminated the darkness full of a tingling tension of the recently erupted conflict. The clinking silence was occasionally interrupted by quiet sobs from the bed in the dark corner of the room.

Alice curled up in a ball on her bed, shrinking from the piercing pain of resentment and fear of the future, oppressive self-pity, bitterness of disappointment, and a feeling of endless loneliness. Her fluffy pillow with embroidered red roses was soaked with tears. Her head was buzzing with tension as it played with the same thoughts over and over again.

Once again, Alice was one-on-one with the harsh reality. No one was around, but the stars and the moon were silently watching from afar as her fate, imprinted in the star tablets, unfolded in its linear duality.

Alice's husband had left several minutes ago. The loud slamming of the main door, followed by the sound of rapidly receding footsteps, struck Alice's heart. She realized that her marriage was over.

"Well, at least I tried," muttered Alice, trying to suppress her feelings of anger and disappointment. She stared, teary-eyed, at the embroidered roses while her overexcited mind continued its inner dialogue.

I cannot stand this life any longer, whispered the voice of frustration, *I am nothing here…He doesn't see me. I am just a piece of furniture, just a part of his monotonous routine where everything is seemingly fine and he is fully satisfied with his life in a bubble. And he yells at me and acts as if I'm crazy every time I want us to change something in our life. Maybe he is afraid of changes, but I cannot live this way…not anymore.*

Then her rational mind jumped in. *What am I going to do? How do I tell him that I want to end our relationship? What will I say to our children? How will I survive on my own?* These thoughts raced through her mind, triggering a wide specter of feelings including fear and guilt.

"Maybe I just need some rest," she reasoned aloud, trying to calm down her out-of-control emotions. "Then things will go back to normal."

Suddenly, as fast as a flash of lightning, a message appeared from nowhere and hit her heart: *You will die if you stay in this relationship.*

"Hmmm…that's true," wistfully replied Alice to the invisible forces that had sent her such a shockingly honest message. "I feel it. Each cell of my body feels that if I change nothing, I will get sick and die soon."

As Alice's children grew up and no longer required much of her attention, she had lost the meaning of her life. She started having to come up with reasons to get up every morning and go to her job or do stuff around the house. She also stopped rushing home after work, because nobody was waiting there for her.

On her way home, she often asked herself, "Is this how I'm supposed to spend the rest of my life? Sleep, work, eat, repeat? What for?"

Alice didn't feel she was wanted, loved, or needed anymore. Instead, she felt like part of the interior design that existed for everyone's convenience and service without being noticed until it was not in its place. She felt that there was no one for her in the whole world. She wondered how she had arrived in this present that felt so lonely?

"What did I do wrong?" she whispered, "Why does nobody love me?"

The powerlessness she felt when such thoughts and emotions boiled, sizzled, and bubbled inside was unbearable. Guilt and innocence, self-confidence and self-doubt, rage and loyalty were locked in an endless battle, each determined to win. Despair and hopelessness responded with an aching feeling in the area of her solar plexus, which made her shrink into a ball. There was no way, at least none she could see, to escape the fight.

A new stream of tears gushed from Alice's beautiful bottomless eyes, restricting her breath. She took out another tissue from the bottom of a box with a colorful unicorn on it and blew her nose loudly. Suddenly, she recalled how her friend Mary taught her to focus on a feeling and follow it as if it were Theseus, the hero of Alice's favorite Greek myth, who followed a string of Ariadne's magical ball of yarn out of the labyrinth.

Alice closed her red, swollen eyes and focused on the painful feeling of loneliness as if it was a silver string vibrating in her heart. She then allowed the string to lead her somewhere in the past. It was pulling Alice into an event where she had experienced similar feelings. One by one, pictures from her past flew in front of her closed eyes.

CHAPTER TWO

Alice's memory brought her to when she was about five years old. In Little Alice's eyes, the world was full of miracles. She loved fairytales and would listen in open-mouthed awe to stories about magnificent dragons that looked like those lizards basking in the sun on a big rock next to the house. She loved *Beauty and the Beast* and discovered that not one but many enchanted roses were growing in their backyard. From their petals, Alice created several outstanding ball gowns for her fairies of flowers.

Little Alice also loved to make a big splash when she jumped into the water. She was mesmerized to watch how her little feet instantly transformed standing water into thousands of sparkly drops that could fly and then disappear, leaving just a wet spot. It was a magical world, and Alice was an almighty magician in it. As she relived this memory, a warm feeling of love for her little self enveloped Alice, and her lips curved into a slight indulgent smile.

But the very next moment, a shadow of bitterness reflected on her face with stiffness and tension. A long-forgotten story began to unfold in Alice's memory.

It had been raining the whole night. Alice woke up early in the morning and could not wait for the sun to show up so she could go outside. Her mom was busy cleaning the house and allowed Alice to play near the home as soon as the first rays of sunlight reached the wet soil.

"Hooray!" exclaimed the little girl. She rushed to put on her yellow rainboots and blue jacket with silvery buttons, then loped by the kitchen, through a small hallway out the door.

Outside, Alice stopped for a moment, enjoying the fresh air and watching how water was still dropping from the oak tree's leaves. Soon, her attention was attracted by the water in the puddles reflecting the blue sky with animal-shaped white clouds. Alice's heart was bouncing with joy and excitement. She could not resist stepping on the cloud's reflection in the widest and deepest puddle to create the biggest splash. It was fun.

After that, she wanted to split the water, watching how the magical waves she created with her feet moved away from each other and reunited again. Alice was surfing her mini ocean back and forth when she noticed a beautiful white flower on the hill. The flower looked so tender and sweet.

The thought, *Mommy would love this flower!* instantly went through Alice's mind. Alice loved her mother from the bottom of her pure heart, and thought this flower was as beautiful as her mom was.

"I should bring it to her," decided the girl.

The plan was made fast. Alice bravely crossed a slippery, muddy hill and reached the white flower. As her small hand confidently plucked it, the image of a smiling mother appeared in her imagination. Now she had to deliver this magic beauty to her mother as fast as possible. Alice rushed back through mud and puddles. She was in a hurry to make her mother happy. Her heart was joyfully pounding in anticipation of seeing her mother soon.

While Alice explored the magical quality of water outside, her mother was finishing her housework. Beads of sweat slowly slid down her forehead. She was tired, but the shiny-clean kitchen floor made her feel good. The mother was thinking about dinner with her husband and daughter and how they would enjoy walking barefoot on such a clean floor.

The mother still was holding the wet rag in her hands when her little daughter burst into the house, screaming, "Mommy, look what I found for you!"

Alice ran to her, holding out a snow-white flower as a symbol of her endless love. "This is for you!" exclaimed Alice joyfully.

When she had nearly crossed the kitchen, her mother's piercing cry of "Stop!" made her freeze in place.

"What are you doing? I just cleaned the floor!" yelled the mother. Her face expressed anger, disappointment, and self-pity at the same time. "Are you blind? Take your dirty boots off…immediately!"

She then pointed to the dirty spots Alice's boots left on the floor. It was as if she, her mother, was Zeus, tossing a lightning bolt from her index finger. A wave of guilt and fear went through the girl's body.

"I spent the whole day making this house clean. But who cares? Nobody appreciates my hard work. You are exactly like your father!"

In her burst of negative emotions, the mother saw neither Alice nor the flower. She fully sunk into a world where she perceived herself as unappreciated by anyone, where she was lonely and unhappy.

Alice stood in the midst of this raging storm, feeling unprotected and completely confused. She could not grasp why her desire to express her love has made her mother mad. Her head sank into her tensed little shoulders as if defending or hiding herself; her tiny fist tightly squeezed the flower's stem.

In that moment a boulder of resentment formed to block the flow of pure love. Her trust was ruined; doubts gave rise to fear that settled in her heart. Alice's eyes were full of tears and a slight shiver went through her little body as she slowly went into the hallway to take her boots off. The magic flower drooped all over and bowed its head in Alice's hands. Bitter tears flowed down Alice's cheeks and dripped onto the white flower, a symbol of rejected love.

With a disgruntled grunt, Alice's mother soaked a rag in a bucket of soapy water and began to mop the floor again. Alice knew nothing about her mother's thoughts and feelings. But that day, she had discovered that an open heart is vulnerable and easy to hurt; a spontaneous expression of love can be punished; the bustle and hustle of the human world are more important than the magical world of nature and love.

Alice never knew that the day following the conflict her mother found a withered flower on a stool by the front door, and her heart ached from the sudden surge of pain. The moment of rage was gone, and she realized how much she had hurt the soul of her loving daughter.

She was filled with remorse but knew the damage had already been done. She could not change the past, but she could try to make amends and reconnect with her daughter. She decided to take Alice to an amusement park and buy her something, but she never made up her mind to talk with Alice about the love that connected them so tightly. She told only one person, her sister Clara, about her deep remorse, but Clara didn't understand her feelings and quickly forgot the story.

Alice opened her eyes and turned to the other side. Her body was numb, and a slight chill ran through her shoulders. She pulled her favorite ivy pink blanket over her. The warmth brought comfort, and Alice was carried back through the waves of memory.

She again pictured herself as a small child and realized that her current feelings of loneliness and powerlessness were rooted in what she had experienced that long-ago day in her childhood home. She recalled how she had sat on the green wooden stool by the front door, holding a white flower in her little hand, and feeling like nobody was there for her.

CHAPTER THREE

As her emotions calmed, Alice's rational mind took the reins of control. She felt so much pity for little Alice.

"Why didn't my parents love me?" she asked, "Why did they hurt my feelings so often?"

Her own heart had always been so full of love and affection for her mother and father. They were her entire world. Looking back, she could see that her parents had been preoccupied with adult things – things that were not understandable for a little girl who desperately needed to feel their love. Because they were so busy, Alice learned she could not crawl onto her mother's lap or play with her father whenever she desired. Oftentimes, she had to wait for what seemed like forever before her mother or father gave their full attention to her.

When Alice thought of her mother, she always had an image of her wearing a sunny yellow shirt with a floral embossed pattern and a brown midi skirt flared down. Her dark hair was pulled back into a short ponytail. Even before she was old enough to speak, Alice noticed that her mother was in constant motion – always cooking, cleaning, and caring for the family.

Alice remembers feeling protected when her mother was in charge and confidently commanded what was happening. She also recalls becoming scared when her mother was at a loss and tried to get support from someone, including Alice herself.

Alice doesn't remember much about her father. Usually, he was either working or relaxing in his chair in front of the TV. Sometimes he was in a playful mood and played with Alice or taught her to do, as he called it, "manly stuff" such as sawing boards, hammering nails, and connecting electrical wires. Though her dad was not constantly on the run like Mom, he was athletic and liked to walk around in black sweatpants and plain t-shirts. He introduced Alice to riding a bicycle and urged her not to cry if she fell.

"You are not a snotty, crying girl," he would say, "You are strong."

Unlike her mother, who constantly was pointing out Alice's imperfections, her father focused on her achievements and often encouraged her to move forward.

"Get up. Try again. You can do it," he told her, and she believed every word.

Each moment she spent with him was so joyful she wished it would never stop.

The little girl was very sensitive to everything that happened in her surroundings. She could also, though she didn't realize it, feel the mood or emotional state of everyone around her. As a result, Alice could become anxious whenever she perceived her father's fear or her mother's resentment and uncertainty. But her parents had never paid much attention to Alice's feelings. They didn't see their daughter's struggle, for the eyes of their souls were always looking somewhere else. Even when Alice fell ill or acted up to get her parents' attention, her sensitive heart knew that though they were physically present, their minds were elsewhere. Though Alice was surrounded by her family, the loneliness and feeling like she didn't belong was what she experienced the most.

Alice learned that her parents had certain expectations about her behavior and choices, and she often found herself playing roles that fit what they wanted her to be. In this way, she was introduced to a world where everyone wears various masks to hide their individuality or to reap some other advantage.

For several years, Alice had heard her mother and father loudly arguing. It was upsetting, but things always settled down… until one evening, they didn't. Instead, her father loaded his dark brown suitcase into the car and drove away without saying a word to Alice. It was as if she didn't even exist. At that moment, Alice's safe, familiar world collapsed.

"What did I do wrong?" she quietly cried.

But nobody could answer her question. Alice's mother was crying and yelling, blaming her husband for her miserable life. The once confident woman was now devastated, vulnerable, and in need of support and protection. She was also blind to her daughter's broken heart.

For Alice, it was a painful realization. There was no hope of her remaining the joyful child, there was no hope of her being loved anymore. Now she was on a secret mission to save her mom, even if she must sacrifice her own purpose and happiness to do so.

At the same time, Alice tried to understand which of her parents was to blame for the separation.

Why did Mom allow that to happen? she'd think, questioning her mom's ability to handle conflicts. *She didn't love him as I do… Yeah, but sometimes he acted weird, especially when he was drunk.*

A picture of the oscillating knife her dad had stabbed furiously into their wooden dining table suddenly surfaced in her mind.

Why did he do that? Anyway, he was kind, and I miss him so much. But why did he leave without talking with me? Does he think about me sometimes?

Alice's eyes filled with tears again. This time, from the loss of connection with her father, whose love lived in her heart no matter what.

With a start, Alice returned to the present. She was no longer a small child, but a grown woman with a spouse and grown children of her own. Exhausted by the stress of the past six hours, the muscles of her body began to relax and her breathing became smoother and deeper. Images of her parents, little Alice, her husband John, and her kids began to rush through her mind.

"How confusing and complicated everything is in this world. Where is love? Does it exist only in fairytales? Can I see the world of magic again?"

Alice yawned. "I'll have to talk to Mary about it." With these thoughts and a strong intention to meet Mary soon, Alice plunged into a dreamland where magic was still possible.

CHAPTER FOUR

Alice crossed the road and accelerated her steps, maneuvering between many pedestrians. There had been a rush at work, and now she was late to meet Mary. An old and dear friend, Mary knew how to present any situation from an unusual perspective. Alice loved listening to her talk about the invisible world of energetic connections. Sometimes it was impossible to understand, yet there was always something mysterious and magical about Mary's stories that drew Alice in.

This time, Alice was seeking an answer to a specific question: how could she get out of the life situation she was currently trapped in?

She ran her hand across her forehead, wiping away the tiny beads of sweat that had formed there during her brisk walk.

Finally, she thought as the terrace of the restaurant came into view. It was Alice and Mary's favorite meeting place. The entire perimeter was planted with all kinds of flowers. Sweet peas curled along the side trails, which provided shade and coziness. Two large clay pots with lush pink hydrangea bushes stood at the entrance to the terrace. Crimson and white-striped petunias hung from hanging baskets.

Mary was seated on a cushioned bench at the table on the right side of the terrace. The table, which was small, round, and covered with a white tablecloth, had a miniature flower arrangement in a small transparent vase in the middle. Mary thoughtfully examined the tender blooms. Occasionally, she stirred the mojito and watched how its bright green mint leaves lazily swirled around the ice cubes. Her movements were relaxed, and the slight, benevolent smile on her face expressed nothing but pleasure.

"Here I am!" cried Alice excitedly while entering the terrace. "I'm so sorry… unexpectedly had to stay late."

Mary stood and the friends embraced each other tenderly.

"I missed you so much," Alice said, still slightly winded from her walk.

"Hi, dear. I'm so happy to see you," said Mary, smiling. "Don't worry. Let's sit down. Catch your breath. Would you like something to drink?"

Alice called the waiter and ordered herself a mojito and a glass of water. Now she could finally relax and calmly look at Mary, whom she had not seen for several months.

"What a beautiful dress," she said, "I love floral patterns. You look stunning."

"Thank you," Mary replied as she watched her friend's fussy movements. She perceived that behind this bustle, there was much more than guilt for being late. She listened carefully, trying to understand what was happening in her friend's heart.

They ordered pizza and salad and made small talk while they waited. They talked about how things were going, each offering the same remarks that everything was fine. They exchanged the latest news about mutual friends and acquaintances, about their children and parents. The conversation glided over the surface, and neither one dared to raise the issue about which Alice was in such a hurry to meet. Then, when they had nearly finished the pizza, Mary suddenly asked, "Alice, what's going on?"

Alice, who had been chattering on about something, fell silent and looked directly at Mary. It seemed her friend's dark, fathomless eyes saw through her and into the corners of her soul. There was nothing more to hide, and Alice burst into tears.

"Mary, dear, I need your help," Alice said with a sob. "I'm confused. I can't live like this anymore and am afraid to change something. I'm stuck and don't know what to do." She paused, wiping her tears and wet nose. "I feel so alone, I'm lost."

She then opened up about her recent conflict with her husband and how she felt like she was dying in this bleak relationship.

"John and I have lived together for almost twenty years, but something is broken in our relationship. Love is gone. I feel as if we became roommates with additional obligations. Everything had become routine, the same one we've had forever. Today was as bleak as yesterday," Alice added, sounding irritated, "and tomorrow will be the same as today.

"I'm dying in this relationship," she continued, "and I don't know what to do. I'm afraid to make a mistake, "I'm scared of the uncertainty. Also, I don't know how our children would take it if we divorced – and what about John?"

Then she expressed concern about her husband's parents, older people with health problems. Who knew what such distressing news would do to them.

Mary silently watched as Alice's thoughts and feelings darted from side to side as wild birds closed in a cage. The sparks of the battles in her friend's eyes periodically lit up and faded away. Internal disagreement to live as before fought with the desire to keep peace in the family, the willingness to change fought with doubts about the future, and the desire to be free fought with the fear of losing belonging. Mary was listening with compassion and patience. She could sense that Alice's inner battle was multi-dimensional. Mary witnessed how each feeling Alice expressed immediately created the contradicting one. Moreover, those initial feelings awakened other feelings that had been suppressed long ago.

In the end, Alice expressed her anger toward herself; her parents, who had raised her incorrectly; her husband, who did not live up to her expectations, and so on. But Mary's calmness helped Alice return from the world of raging feelings about the past and the future into the reality of here and now.

"Sometimes, I think maybe I've made this all up in my head, that I can take it," Alice said thoughtfully. "I'm scared to think I could hurt so many people. I cannot do that."

"I see," said Mary. "I have just one question for you."

Alice lifted her tear-stained eyes and looked at Mary with interest.

"You are a good daughter, a great wife, a wonderful mother. You just said how important it is to you that everyone is well cared for and happy. I sincerely admire you. And now I want to ask yourself, who is supposed to take care of Alice?" Mary paused. "Who will take care that your soul fulfills its destiny? Who is supposed to fill your soul with joy?"

Alice's almond-shaped eyes widened in surprise. No one had ever asked about her soul before. It had also never crossed her mind to think about it.

"Who...?" Alice repeated, her dumbfounded mind beginning to analyze the situation. It became crystal clear that there was only one person in the whole world who was in charge of the well-being of her soul. It was her, Alice. Then, suddenly, everything began to fall into place. The heaviness in her chest magically disappeared, and Alice felt like she could breathe again. She sighed with relief, and the veil of sadness lifted from her face.

Evening came all too quickly. The streetlights were lit, shading the brightness of the stars with their intensity. It was time to go home. Alice did not receive all the answers, but she felt that Mary's last question provoked some internal shift that needed space and time to fully be realized.

"Thank you for this meeting. I appreciate you so much." Alice paused. "I still need your wisdom, though. May I call you this Saturday?"

"Yes, of course. I'm always happy to talk to you. Call me on Saturday afternoon," said Mary.

The girlfriends hugged goodbye and wished each other good night. Mary hurried into the yellow cab she had ordered in advance, and Alice slowly wandered to the bus stop. She enjoyed the coolness of the evening, the night-scented fragrance of Matthiola longipetala hanging from people's balconies, and thought about her forgotten soul. Surprisingly though, these thoughts brought sincere relief and inner peace, which Alice needed.

CHAPTER FIVE

That Saturday, Alice sat in a cozy, dark blue velour armchair by the open window. Though it was summertime, it was cool outside, and gusts of fresh air periodically burst into the room, bringing the aromas of flowering acacias. Alice shivered a little and wrapped herself more tightly in the lilac shawl lying on her narrow shoulders. The wind playfully stirred the dense crowns of trees, and Alice watched a magical action of light and shadows, where rays of sunlight made their way here and there through the green foliage, and fussy birds loudly carried on their conversation.

Alice held the phone tightly in her hand and listened carefully to Mary's melodious voice.

"Have you spoken to John about your decision?" Mary asked gently.

"Not yet," Alice replied quietly, almost ashamedly. "I still can't decide."

"It's okay. Any fruit must be ripe to be enjoyed. The right time will come. Listen to your heart and watch for a sign from the Universe. "

"Okay," Alice said, for she trusted her friend even if she didn't always trust the Universe.

"I just need to be certain that I am doing the right thing," exhaled Alice.

"Do you remember the story of Adam and Eve?" Mary asked.

"Vaguely," Alice replied, puzzled by the abrupt shift in topic. "Why?"

"You know that they were enjoying their immortal life in the Garden of Eden…"

Alice thought, *How can she always bring up such unusual topics and find connections others would never notice?*

Alice knew that Mary had developed her intuition and loved to reflect on stories she learned from books or her surroundings, especially her job, where she interacted with many people. After her children set off on their own life journeys and her husband lost a battle with a terminal illness, Mary started spending even more time reading, meditating, and attending different seminars where she could connect with those invisible forces that govern the Universe.

One of the things Alice liked most about Mary was that she didn't seek to change the imperfections of the world she observed or the people she was around. She instead focused on searching for who she was and tried to accept her own dark sides. Surprisingly, the world started to change in tandem with her transformation, which inspired Mary to explore this metamorphosis in depth, and she was happy to take her friends along for the journey.

"The garden was full of beautiful trees," Mary continued, "including the Tree of Life and the Tree of Knowledge. They had always had everything needed for a carefree, happy existence."

The image of a beautiful divine garden unfolded in Alice's imagination.

"Adam and Eve were allowed to eat from any tree in the garden except the Tree of Knowledge. The apples from the prohibited tree were so attractive that they couldn't resist trying them."

Alice easily pictured that magical tree standing alone in the meadow, attracting everyone with the brightness of its juicy fruits.

"So, they decided to taste the fruit of the forbidden tree, and suddenly, their perception of the world changed, and they looked at each other with judgmental eyes. In a blink of an eye, their perfect world split into two polarized worlds, and their innocence was replaced with guilt."

Mary paused.

"The story tells that because of their action, Adam and Eve become sinners, so the Lord God banished them from the Garden. Moreover, they lost their access to the Tree of Life. Since then, the offspring of Adam and Eve have lived in a world of duality where everything is divided into good and evil. As a result, each of us is involved in an endless, exhausting fight between deep-seated beliefs about right and wrong and between the desire for freedom and the need to belong. Ironically," Mary said in conclusion, "the goal of this struggle is to achieve peace and justice."

"What a sad story," said Alice.

"Don't you think it reflects our reality?" Mary asked. "In my perception, each of us arrives in this world as a miracle of wholeness and holiness carried by the flow of love. Each of us is blessed with unique talents and creative power. Unfortunately, nobody remembers that. We mostly focus on our faults or someone else's instead of supporting our natural skills and talents."

Alice imagined the day she was taken on her first ride from the hospital where she was born to the house that became her home for a few decades. She imagined how her mother was sitting in the back seat, cuddling her beautiful baby girl. Alice's bright dark blue eyes radiated nothing but pure love. When she smiled, everyone smiled in response with tenderness in their heart. Alice was a perfect creation of divine nature. She could feel the well-known heartbeat of her mother and hear her voice, which brought comfort and a feeling of safety.

When her mother was around, Baby Alice's new world was as complete as the Divine Garden of Eden. Her clear perception of the world did not distinguish between good and evil. In a state of oneness with the whole world, Alice observed herself as part of the world, smiling and speaking of herself in the third person.

But after a while, Alice's caregivers began to feed the child with the fruit of knowledge, teaching her to distinguish between good and evil. Her world started splitting, often triggering painful feelings and emotions. Like her ancient ancestors before they ate from the Tree of Knowledge, she was not ashamed of her nakedness. There was no doubt in a baby's Alice undeveloped mind that she was good, just as she was.

Mary's voice interrupted Alice's flow of thoughts, "On the way to the material world, we first separate from the divine world of infinity. Then, we detach from our mother. After that, we have a life-long battle while creating and cutting inner and outer connections to understand that each separation is excruciating." Alice was carefully listening and felt that it was true for her life.

By age ten, Alice's perception of the world dramatically changed, and the carefree smile disappeared from her face. An inner judge was established to decide what was right and wrong, and the gate of Eden shut behind her.

"Does it mean there is no way to find love and peace in this crazy world?" asked Alice.

"One who seeks will always find," responded Mary. "But few are willing to risk going in search."

"Why?" asked Alice.

"Because at the beginning of the journey, you must leave your old, well-established ideas about yourself and the world in the past and open yourself to new possibilities. Like Moses, who had to take off his sandals standing on the holy ground in front of the Burning Bush, you have to let go of everything that prevents you from moving into a new realm. After that, you must learn to trust the Universe that is always with you to overcome the fear of an unknown future."

"Will I find love and get rid of loneliness if I follow this path?" asked Alice.

"It all depends on you. You may reopen the love and freedom that has always existed within. Then your perception of loneliness will change."

Alice thought for a moment. "Do you think I can do that?"

"I believe that everyone can do it. It's your life, and you can choose whatever you want to do with it. It's always about your choice."

"Choices…that is what makes me so anxious," said Alice. "How do I know if my choice is right?"

"It depends on who the judge is."

"What do you mean?"

"Well, let me explain it briefly," said Mary. "Our mind-body-spirit operates in different realms simultaneously. Your body is the bridge between the visible and invisible worlds. I see it as a wise, self-regulating system that serves your needs while your soul is in its divine mission in this physical world. The body doesn't use words to judge your choices. However, it may send you signals via pain or other symptoms when you make choices that can harm your physical shell – for example, a headache after a wild drinking party.

Your soul may signal if you deviate too much from your soul's designation based on your choices. In this case, you may feel a deep dissatisfaction akin to longing for something unknown without having any reasonable explanation for this feeling. Your body shares this feeling with you, but it's beyond your mind's understanding.

"The biggest and the most controversial court resides in your mind. This head's office records everything that happened in the past, present, and imaginable future; it edits and re-records all events every time you recall them; it creates billions of possible imaginable connections between events while it tries to make sense out of everything. If there is an event with no logical explanation, your mind will exclude it.

"For example, all world scientists can prove the fact that about ninety-nine percent of my body is made mostly of water or atoms of hydrogen, carbon, nitrogen, and oxygen. But my mind does not accept this idea…at least not now. This is not how I see myself in a mirror or how others see me.

'And because I don't know myself, I listen to others, starting with my parents, about who I am. Eventually, other people's ideas about me form a network of invisible judges who control each step and my decisions. We call it the belief system. This is where all the crazy dramas and bloody wars come from."

Mary fell silent then, and for a moment Alice thought the call had dropped.

"Hello! Are you there?"

"Yes, I am here," Mary said, then paused for another beat. "Would you like to join me for a workshop that my friend Sara is holding in two weeks? It includes a seminar that you might appreciate."

"What kind of workshop?" asked Alice.

"It's a Family Constellation seminar. Sara learned about this profound work from Bert Hellinger, a German philosopher who introduced it about twenty years ago. This is a very unusual workshop because it is experiential… probably that is why it's so hard to explain."

"I've never attended such a seminar," confessed Alice. "How does it work?"

"Well, first of all, I believe this seminar is for people who are brave enough to explore a world of hidden dynamics and face the truth…" Mary paused. "…the truth about where one's love flows or is stuck. Any participant may ask to set a constellation for his or her issue. For example, if you want to look at your situation with your husband, you can ask Sara to set a constellation for you. You just need to formulate your request very clearly and concisely."

"Should I share with the whole group my story?" asked Alice.

"No, absolutely not!" said Mary. "That is why I love these workshops. You don't have to share anything except the most basic facts — for example, about the number of kids you have. Sara told me that the less everybody knows about a person they represent, and about the client, is better."

"Why is that?"

"I think it prevents representatives from making assumptions about what they're supposed to feel. Representatives should follow the inner movements that they perceive through their bodies. When you know nothing about a person you represent, it's easy for you to turn your judgmental mind off."

Mary paused, and Alice could hear the sound of metal delicately hitting glass as Mary stirred her herbal tea. "Honestly, nobody can clearly explain how it works." She paused again for a sip, then added with both bewilderment and conviction, "But it does work…"

"Mary, I have to admit, this is the first time I do not understand your explanation," said Alice.

"Exactly!" Mary exclaimed and burst out laughing. "That's why I said that in order to understand it you have to try it. But I will tell you what I witnessed during Sara's last seminar.

"A woman, I believe her name was Rosa, wanted to know why her eleven-year-old son misbehaved and at times was extremely angry at her. Neither she nor her husband knew how to deal with the boy. Sara said that children portray family dynamics, as they are more sensitive to them. Then, she asked two men and a woman to represent Rosa's family. She watched as Rosa's representative and the representative for her husband looked at each other for a few moments and then slowly turned their backs on each other. Neither one looked at the representative of their son. The son's representative first looked at his "father," then turned and followed his father's gaze. The mother's representative, as I mentioned before, was looking in the opposite direction."

Mary paused as if trying to recall the rest.

"Yeah… that's right. The 'parents' didn't look at their 'son.' Their love was flowing somewhere else…

"This was a very dramatic moment. The audience was so quiet and focused, as if it was their own situation. Sara watched each movement of the representatives, and when movements froze, she asked each parent if they'd had a significant other before they came together. Both of them said yes, and Sara added representatives for their former partners.

"The moment the mother saw the representative of her former boyfriend, her face lit up and her eyes radiated so much love…it just flew like a river toward him. The 'boy,' in the meantime, was staring at the father's former girlfriend, who was clenching her fists in anger. Then he made one tiny step toward her, then another, and finally, he stood next to the woman and looked in the direction of his parents.

"Sara explained that on the soul level the boy could feel these dynamics and was expressing his father's former partner's rage toward his mother. Rosa began nodding in agreement with what was happening. She put her hands on the heart area and tears ran over her face. To me, it was as if her eyes came in tune with her soul's eyes, and the truth revealed itself," said Mary.

"So, what happened next?" Alice asked, completely enthralled.

"Sara allowed the parents' representatives to have eye contact with their former partners. Also, I remember that she asked the father to express his gratitude to his former girlfriend for all the good he received from her or because of her. After that, the woman unclenched her fists, and a half-smile appeared on her face. At some point, both parents' representatives embraced their former partners, and after a while the mother and father faced each other smiling and looked at their son, who was looking at them with love."

"Unbelievable," said Alice when Mary had finished her story. "Did it help Rosa?"

"I think so. Rosa saw the truth. She got a new perspective that was very different from all the stories and explanations she had before, and it made an inner shift that may lead to changes. Also, I believe her son was relieved," added Mary.

"Impressive…" Alice said with a combination of enthusiasm and hope. "It sounds like we can fix all our problems by doing family constellations?"

"I don't think so," giggled Mary. "It doesn't 'fix' your problems, but it does help you develop a wider perspective on the circumstances of your life and become more flexible so you can withstand the storms."

"Well, I'm definitely interested," Alice said, "Email me the details and I'll let you know if I can be there."

"Will do." Mary replied, "I love you."

"I love you too. Talk to you later. Bye."

I should talk to John this Wednesday evening when the children go to play basketball, Alice thought as she hung up the phone.

CHAPTER SIX

John was sitting in the corner of the couch, holding a dark green beer bottle in his hand and watching with a tightened jaw as the dogfight unfolded on the TV screen. He was so involved in what was happening that his body leaned forward and his head stretched father still, as if he could help the pilot avoid a fatal shot.

The delicious smells of roasted meat and vegetable soup wafted in from the kitchen.

"Dinner is ready," said Alice, and recognized the feeling of irritation that rose within her.

Her husband was in a different reality. He fought alongside the hero pilot, and everything else, including Alice's presence, remained outside his awareness.

"Are you going to join me for dinner?" asked Alice again. There was a hint of displeasure in her voice.

"This is the most important part," he replied, "Start serving the dinner. I'll be there in a few minutes."

His last words added fuel to the fire.

Now, I will tell him everything, she thought as she ladled the fragrant soup into a bowl. *It feels like a never-ending déjà vu. It can't go on like this anymore. Let him live with his TV and hire a housekeeper.*

Alice picked up bowl, now hot from the steaming soup. It burned her fingers as she rushed to put it on the table without spilling a drop. So many times she had served a meal to her family in this bowl! They had received this set of china as a wedding gift. The golden edging was worn off in some places, but Alice loved the subtle dark blue geometric pattern that framed the plates. It triggered a feeling of nostalgia.

We used to have such a good time together. What happened?

"Okay, ready," John announced as he walked into the kitchen with a gleeful smile. The smile drooped a bit when he glanced at her.

"Why are you so gloomy? Something happened?"

All was well in John's world. He could not even imagine what a devastating storm of change was gathering over his head.

"This looks great," he said without waiting for an answer to his question. "...and with fresh parsley..."

He looked at the table, for the first time noticing there were only two place settings. "Where are the children?" he asked, then lightly tapped his forehead with his palm. "Right, today is Wednesday. Well, sit down… let's eat."

His childish openness, and his lack of any suspicion that something was wrong between them, made Alice doubt her decision.

By and large, he's a good person. It's just that I don't want to be with him anymore. Maybe I want too much from him? Then she remembered all the times she had told him that things needed to change, that their relationships needed to change as their life circumstances had. She also remembered how he had yelled at her, saying that everything was perfect and she was making drama out of nothing.

She looked at John, who seemed to be thinking about something as he slowly sipped his soup.

"It's delicious," he said with a glance at Alice, then he sunk into his thoughts again. Every time his cell phone's screen lit up, he checked the messages but didn't read them.

"I want to talk to you," Alice began timidly.

John tore his eyes from his bowl and looked at her.

"I have already told you we need to change something in our lives…"

"This again…" he replied, immediately annoyed. "So, what do you want?"

Alice was trying to gather her thoughts and find the right words when John's phone rang. A picture of her mother-in-law appeared on the screen.

"Wait a minute," said John. "Probably something happened there if Mom's calling at this time."

Alice let out a sigh. She could hear her mother-in-law's voice speaking quickly and unintelligibly to John. Concern appeared on John's face.

"Okay, don't worry. I'll come over and sort it out. Yes, fine. See you soon." John ended the call and got up from the table.

"What happened?" Alice asked.

"Dad climbed up to change a light bulb and he fell. Now he can't stand on his left leg because of the pain, and Mom is worried that he has a fracture. Her blood pressure went up due to nerves. You know her. She panics over nothing." He paused. "Will you go with me?"

"Of course," Alice replied. Clearly, her announcement that she wanted to separate was not going to happen now.

Not today... again, not today... thought Alice while putting on her favorite silvery sandals. She then grabbed the small bag filled with everything she needed for all occasions and hurried after John, who was already waiting for her near the car.

CHAPTER SEVEN

The workday was drawing to a close. The sounds of doors being shut and the steps of employees hurrying out could be heard from the corridor. Alice stood by the massive window in her office on the twenty-third floor and watched the movement of tiny cars and people along the streets adjacent to the skyscraper. Everyone seemed to have a goal and an understanding of where they needed to go. Even the birds and clouds flying outside the window knew the direction of their movement. Only Alice did not know what to do next. Suddenly she remembered that her former colleague Bella had suggested they meet for coffee sometime. Bella now worked at a nearby bank, and though they had not communicated in a long while, Alice knew she liked to unwind after work at L'amour, a coffee shop around the corner. Maybe she'd be available tonight…

Without hesitation, Alice grabbed her phone, found Bella's name on her contact list and pressed the call button. Indeed, Bella was surprised and very excited to hear from her – and get the latest gossip at her former place of employment. They agreed to meet in twenty minutes at L'amour.

Alice was the first to arrive and took a table for two by a window framed with heavy, grass-colored drapery. Despite the evening influx of people, the atmosphere was relaxing and inviting. Music played softly, and someone sang an old French chanson. Although Alice had never been to France, the sound of this music, small openwork tables, and pictures of Parisian sights hanging on the walls created the illusion that she was in Paris for a moment.

Alice was telling the waiter that she was waiting for a friend when Bella's curvaceous form appeared in the doorway. Her face lit up when she saw Alice and quickly moved toward her with arms open wide.

Alice stood and the friends exchanged a quick hug.

"I'm so happy you called!" Bella said as she sat down. "Unfortunately, I can't stay long today. I have to be home by nine." She asked the waiter to bring her hot chocolate, camembert, and fruit salad.

"So tell me...how are you? How is your family, work?" Bella began to ask questions with unconcealed interest.

"Work is good," Alice replied with a smile. "I recently got promoted to head of the department."

"Wow, congratulations! I'm so happy for you." Bella eyed her outfit appreciatively. "You definitely look the part." Then, without missing a beat, she asked, "Are you hiring? My son is graduating from university soon and looking for a job."

Alice drew back in surprise. "Nick is already graduating from university? "I remember when you brought him to the office like it was yesterday... He was wearing blue shorts and holding a clockwork car that for some reason kept falling and that made you upset." Alice's smile faded. "My kids, too, will soon fly out of the nest," she said with a note of sadness.

"Yeah, time flies fast. I can't get away with a clockwork car anymore. Now he wants a fancy sports car." Bella grinned. "But seriously, let me know if you need anyone. He is a brilliant guy." Bella sighed. "Of course, he gets angry when he finds out I am trying to promote him. Sometimes he yells at me, thinking that I control him too much and get involved in his affairs. But you know... a mother always wants good things for her child."

"It's true. Only lately, I can't seem to tell the difference between good and bad," said Alice.

Bella looked at her friend in surprise, but before she could say anything the waiter's arrival diverted her attention. Bella's eyes grew wide with delight when he gracefully set down a large mug of hot chocolate with a generous dollop of whipped cream lightly sprinkled with cocoa. This was followed by two slices of baguette, cheese, and fruit in an elegant crystal rosette.

For Alice, he brought a layered croissant with a crispy crust, delicious creamy filling, and coffee in a small cup on a saucer with an openwork pattern.

The smell of warm rolls, chocolate, and coffee enveloped the women with its cozy warmth.

Bella sipped her hot chocolate and closed her eyes in pleasure.

"That's good," she said, then set the mug down and reached for a cheese baguette. "But what do you mean, you can't tell the difference between good and bad…?"

"Well, some things that seem to be good are not good for us." She smiled. "I don't drink hot chocolate. It's delicious, but my body doesn't tolerate cocoa for some reason. For me, it's not good."

Bella looked at Alice with a puzzled expression, not sure what hot chocolate had to do with the topic.

"And recently," Alice continued, "I was faced with the fact that I don't know what is good for my children, husband, or myself.

"And it's not just me. My friend Tara is going through the same thing. Tara always doted on her daughter. She treated her like a delicate flower, trying to protect her from unnecessary stress whenever possible. The fact is that the girl had a very vulnerable nervous system, and she was quickly overexcited. Tara sometimes allowed the girl to stay at home and not participate in school activities when she saw that her daughter was on the verge of a nervous breakdown due to these activities.

"Anyway, Tara told me that her daughter takes every opportunity to blame her for being too gentle with her. According to her daughter, it's Tara's fault that she can't succeed in her career!"

Bella stared at her with wide eyes, the piece of baguette with cheese forgotten.

"You always hear stories about bad mothers who beat up their children or didn't care about them," she said... "But for good moms to be bad too...?"

Bella paused and took a sip of her drink. "Your friend raised a selfish daughter. She should have driven her daughter to school, rather than babysitting her."

Then, to Alice's surprise, Bella suddenly became angry.

"You lose sleep worrying about them. You work day and night to get them what they need. You deny yourself everything. And this is the result. Mom is bad."

"Come on, Bella," Alice said soothingly. "This isn't about you." She smiled. "Everything is fine in your world – you own a house, have a job, a brilliant son, and a caring husband. Why are you getting upset?"

"Nothing is good," Bella replied bitterly. "Fred has been cheating on me with his secretary for a long time. I pretend I don't know anything but roar into my pillow every night. My son has become my sole focus – the meaning of life. I was ready to do anything for him. But the more I show concern, the more he gets angry and shuts me out!"

"I'm so sorry, Bella," Alice said, feeling guilty for bringing all this up, "I thought you were fine." She paused. "Have you ever considered divorce?"

"No, never," Bella hastily answered, and fright flashed in her eyes. "A bad husband is better than no husband, and who would want to marry me, a middle- aged woman? Men want beautiful, slender young women. Look at me …"

Bella spread her arms wide and looked down at her body.

Alice looked closely at her friend. Bella had a delicate oval face, beautiful chocolate-colored eyes with tiny rays of wrinkles at the corners, and full lips that showed her softness and kindness. Her full bosom rose with each breath, beckoning with its generous warmth.

"I don't know where you got these ideas from," Alice said. "You are a gorgeous, intelligent woman who still has many choices in life."

"What are you talking about? If I get divorced, I could lose everything – my house, the opportunity to travel and buy expensive things." Bella shook her head. "And what would I be left with? Alone, not needed by anyone, in a rented apartment? And if Nick also leaves … No, it's better not to think about it."

Suddenly a spark of hope appeared in Bella's eyes. "Fred once hinted that I should go to the gym," she whispered. "Maybe if I get back in shape I'll be more attractive to him, and he will love me again."

She stabbed a piece of peach with her miniature dessert fork and popped it into her mouth.

As Alice listened to her friend, indignation began to boil inside her. She had disliked Fred from the moment she met him at a corporate party several years earlier. She remembered his deep-set cold eyes, hooked, thin nose, and sarcastic smile. There was something so arrogant about him, even repulsive.

Does he think he's so great when he looks in the mirror? she thought angrily. *I would immediately break up with a man who said I should change my appearance to keep his love.*

At the same moment, Alice realized that John had never requested anything like that. For the first time in a long time, gratitude for him warmed her heart.

Bella swallowed the peach and stuck her fork into another. "Anyway, I feel good when my husband goes with me somewhere. I am a married woman, and I like it. I am not ready to destroy the life I have, imperfect as it is, in exchange for something I cannot even imagine. I just pray things don't get any worse."

"I see," said Alice as she sipped her cold coffee. "At least you know what you want, and that's great."

CHAPTER EIGHT

Later, as she waited at the bus stop, Alice thought about Bella's words. She would never understand how her wonderful friend could live so many years with such an unattractive and rude man.

She suddenly remembered something Mary had told her: that when two people meet and decide to tie their fate, it is not just their decision. On an invisible plane, two lineages of ancestors decide to unite through their offspring to resolve something that needs to be fixed or healed in their family systems. Mary said each family is like a closed system, maintaining boundaries that isolate it from its surroundings. The only way to bring new energy, ideas, and development into that closed system is to let a person from another family become a member.

Maybe John and I have already solved the problems that our family systems wanted us to fix, and there is no longer a need for us to be together... thought Alice. *Then again, who knows?*

A red bus with yellow stripes pulled to a stop before her and opened the doors. Alice showed the driver her travel card and grabbed a seat near the window just behind him, her thoughts still on the conversation with her friend.

How does Bella endure such disrespect? she thought.

Alice imagined how upset she would be if someone said that to her. Then she realized that she *was* upset, as if it was happening to her. *Why is this situation getting me so wound up?* she wondered.

To analyze her reaction, Alice decided to use the method that had worked for her before: diving into her past, to that dungeon where her painful feelings and emotions had been locked away. Eventually, they sent signals of wanting to be freed, and it seemed her reaction to the conversation with Bella was one of those signals.

The bus swayed evenly, lulling Alice fell into a half-sleep. She saw herself, about fifteen years old, in front of a big mirror hanging on the wall of her dimly lit room, examining her body from head to toe. Her mother was still at work, and there was a deafening silence in the house. Nobody was around. Just a beam of sunlight passed through a crystal on a windowsill, creating a tiny rainbow in the corner of the mirror.

Alice was of medium height and athletic build. Her brown hair, not thick but always well-groomed, fell to her shoulders. From under the long bangs shone beautiful eyes full of sadness. Her beautifully shaped lips twisted into an ironic smile. Alice was upset. Her judgmental thoughts pushed her into a painful confrontation with who she was.

Everyone but me has a boyfriend. What's wrong with me?

Alice's mind searched for an explanation, and her beauty, or lack thereof, seemed the most logical place to start.

I could be more attractive if I was taller and had longer legs, she thought, with her rational mind quickly pointing out that there was nothing she could do about that.

I hate these ugly freckles. No wonder nobody likes me, continued her inner critic. *But you cannot get rid of your skin,* added her mind.

If only I had thick eyelashes over blue eyes and blond hair like Kayla has, Alice thought, picturing the most popular girl in class. *Well, you can color your hair,* her mind conceded, *but you cannot change the color of your eyes.*

As the light shifted, the tiny rainbow in the corner of the mirror slowly dissipated, but not so Alice's negative judgments. Her inability to become as beautiful as somebody else was perceived as a tragedy.

Nearly as painful was the fact that nobody could understand Alice's problem.

"I don't know what you're talking about," said her schoolmate Rosa. "You are gorgeous. And I wish I could be as athletic as you are."

Alice's mother was far harsher when Alice expressed dissatisfaction with her appearance. "Your problems are ridiculous. There are many real issues in the world. Find a job and focus on some of them."

Both in their own way may have been trying to help, but they didn't. Alice felt she was not loved because she was not as good as others who, in her perception, were adored by everyone who knew them – and even by those who didn't.

If only she could be as beautiful as one of those girls on magazine covers and romantic movies. Then she would receive the attention and love she so desperately needed so much. Then her inner judge would step in, saying,

"But you are ugly. That is why nobody loves you."

Alice found her own ideas about herself in her reflection, never seeing her beauty and uniqueness.

The bus braked sharply at a traffic light, jerking Alice fully awake and stopping the flow of self-deprecating thoughts. There were three more stops before home, and she closed her eyes again. But now, her thoughts flowed in a different direction.

Nobody loves…? Wait – who is this "nobody" whose lack of love made me so miserable? Whose love and approval do I keep searching for?

At that moment, an answer came to Alice from the depth of her heart and tears welled up in her eyes. It was the love of her mother and father.

It's not just you, said her inner voice, *Many look for love and appreciation from partners or other people as they become adults to compensate for unfulfilled love in childhood.*

Alice was reminded of her father-in-law, who always behaved like a small child in the presence of his wife. This memory brought a grin to Alice's face.

Can we blame our parents for our feeling unloved? As much as we can blame ourselves for our inability to express love in a way that those around us can feel…

"Mary was right," she whispered. Nobody knew where our souls' eyes turn and where our passion flows.

Alice got off the bus. The street was deserted and dark. Heavy low clouds covered the sky, and somewhere in the distance lightning flashed, followed shortly by thunder. Alice quickened her pace.

I hope John is asleep by the time I go to bed, thought Alice, shuddering at the very idea of intimacy with her husband. Recently, his touches and kisses had disgusted her.

"It's time to finish this story," she said, trying to convince herself.

"It's time to finish this story," she said, trying to convince herself.

CHAPTER NINE

"The mind divides reality into pieces," Sara said, "to be able to analyze them and then connect those pieces in a linear cause-effect chain of logic missing all existing, multidimensional connections. Without perceiving the whole, the mind creates doubts. Doubts create fear. Fear creates resistance and aggression."

Alice was sitting in a white plastic chair next to Mary. About ten more people, mostly women she had never met before, were sitting on either side of her in a large semi-circle. This arrangement allowed the workshop participants to see each other while seated and move freely around the room when Sara suggested they participate in the exercise.

"There is an ancient Indian parable," Sara continued, "about blind wanderers who met something on their way and tried to determine what blocked their path by touch. One wanderer said that he wrapped his arms around a rough but soft column; another stated that he was holding a giant fan; the third determined that a hard spear fell into his hands; the fourth said he was holding something like a hose. Each of them believed he was right and defended his opinion.

"The elephant stood calmly and in bewilderment, watched the blind elders, who held him by different parts of the body and argued loudly." Sara stopped and smiled, looking at the audience.

For Alice, all this was new and incomprehensible, but interesting.

"And now I want to offer you an experiment," said Sara. Alice looked at Mary with excitement.

"We are blind like those elders from the parable. We look at people but don't see them," said Sara. "But you shouldn't take my word for it…" she said, smiling again, "You must get your own experience."

Sara asked all the workshop participants to stand in a circle. Everyone had to make sure that people they did not know were standing on either side of them. Mary gave up her place next to Alice to a good-looking, tall young man with a mop of thick blond hair on his head. To Alice's right was a petite woman. Next, Sara asked the group to walk, making one circle to the left, then to the right. The movement helped relieve any internal tension they felt from not understanding what was happening. Indeed, the mind always demands an explanation, and right now Alice's mind was convinced that all these exercises were complete nonsense and these people were a little bit strange.

After they had stopped moving, Sara asked them to form pairs with the person next to them and make eye contact while observing the sensations in the body. Alice turned to her right and found herself face to face with the small woman, whose face was blushing brightly.

Suddenly, Alice felt a spasm in her throat and her eyes welled with tears that she tried unsuccessfully to suppress. She had no explanation for her body's reaction to a woman she didn't know at all. The woman appeared unmoved; she was just standing there expressionless, breathing deeply. With each breath, her large breasts heaved upward, riveting Alice's gaze to her.

"Grandma..." Alice whispered.

Before her eyes, the image of her grandmother, who died a few years ago, floated up. The spasm tightened her throat even more. She vividly recalled that rare, precious feeling of infinite love and security whenever her grandmother pressed Alice to her ample chest.

Alice was stunned by the experience. She couldn't say how long the experiment took and breathed a sigh of relief when Sara asked everyone to return to their seats. Alice slowly walked across the room to her chair, still thinking about her grandmother. When those who wished to began sharing their experiences, Alice was stunned to learn that most had also "seen" someone other than the stranger beside them. With a start, she realized that when interacting with people, our mind operates from its ideas about that person. Moreover, it doesn't take into consideration that any person changes much faster than our established ideas about them.

Sara's soft voice brought Alice back to the room.

"Several years ago, I watched the movie *Avatar* and Na'vi's words "I see you" inspired me. Shortly thereafter, I was invited to give a short lesson at a local church and decided to talk about this topic. I encouraged people to slow down and look into each other's eyes. It was a chance for everyone to see and be seen with acceptance and understanding." Sara half-smiled. "It did not go well.

"Honestly, I never imagined that people who had known each other for many years and hugged each other every Sunday morning would be so afraid of making eye contact! Later, I learned that some people believe eye contact is an expression of aggression. Some feared something unknown and didn't want to lose control of the situation. And I do understand that. I also understand how our expectations can make us upset and disappointed." She smiled. "It was a good lesson for me: don't make any assumptions."

"Anyway, self-exploration requires enormous courage. Not everyone wants to know the truth, because it might require actions that may lead to changes."

Hearing these words, a chill ran over Alice's skin.

"And what did your experience show you?" she asked the group. "That we could see another person as a mirror in which we can see a reflection of something present in ourselves. This allows us to face the pain we try to avoid with all our might. That is the main reason we avoid eye contact with others; however, it is a way to find understanding and connection between human beings. This is a way towards love and peace."

Sara's gaze went around the circle as she asked the following questions:

"Many life partners believe that they see each other. Is that true? Ask your partner if they feel seen when you look at them." She paused.

"Many children think that they see their parents. Really? Ask your parents if they feel seen when you look at them. And, one more question…the tricky one. Can you see yourself?"

Smiling, Sara again looked around at everyone.

Sara's questions pulled Alice into that distant past when she and John couldn't get enough of each other. They'd looked into each other's eyes for a long time, which gave each of them a deep sense of unity and mutual understanding without words. Their love circulated through their eyes into their hearts and vice versa. But at some point, they had stopped looking into each other's eyes, and now they didn't even look in each other's direction. In fact, Alice tried to remember looking into *anyone's* eyes recently and could not recall one instance.

"If you want to revive your relationship, have a weekly ten-to-fifteen-minute session of eye contact. Discover if you can see each other. Actually, everyone can feel if the person looking at them sees them or is hovering somewhere in their own thoughts. We need to consciously tune into our feelings to widen our perception. When doing this exercise, do not expect anything. Give yourself and your partner a gift of loving attention. Try to see each other, and do not be upset if you discover that one or both of you cannot be fully present and see. Just keep trying."

Sara paused for a beat, then said, "Now, children are another matter. Children do not need eye contact, or the lack thereof, to feel when their parents' love does not reach them. Their perception is not yet blocked by the rational mind.

"Many parents think that they see their children. But is that true?" Sara looked around the group. "Ask your children, and don't be surprised by what you hear. A bunch of toys or money cannot replace a child's need for loving attention."

The group quietly hung on Sara's every word, but the storm of conflicting thoughts and feelings was palpable.

"If children's souls could cry, we would hear everywhere in the air, 'Mom, see me!'" Sara exclaimed passionately.

CHAPTER TEN

"I'm so confused," Alice said as she stirred sugar into her latte. After more exercises Sara announced a break, and she and Mary had decided to go out for a light snack. Fortunately, there was a coffee shop three hundred feet down the street, on the edge of a lush green park, where friends found a quiet space to relax and chat.

"How so?" Mary asked, smiling.

"I mean, how does this work? In the constellation where I was asked to represent the client's mother, I actually felt a deep love for the representative of the daughter, even though I knew nothing about her. I don't even know anything about the woman who asked Sara to set up the constellation!" Alice shook her head, "I know, you told me that when you asked me to go to the seminar, but really? I mean, I just met all these people three hours ago!"

She took a sip of the latte and found it to be delicious.

"And then there was the man Sara placed on my right, who represented the client's father. At first, he did not evoke any emotions in me at all. Then, suddenly, out of nowhere, there was a desire to step away from him. For no reason, I felt hostility, and even I would say anger toward him. Also, for no reason, I started limping when I stepped toward the representative of my daughter."

Mary attentively listened to Alice's every word but said nothing.

"I assume this is how the real mother felt about her daughter and her husband – which was exciting to experience but very hard to comprehend. How am I picking up on these feelings that are not my own?"

Alice paused as she tried to find the right words to describe her experience. "It was as if I was humming my song and at the same time I could hear that somewhere in the neighborhood someone else was humming too. And though she was singing her own song, it touched my feelings no less than my own. How is that possible?"

"You got it!" Mary said happily. "I'm so glad you allowed yourself to feel." She smiled. "You know, you are very sensitive. You even perceived the physical conditions of the woman you represented. I also was surprised when Sara's client shared that her mother limped in real life."

"Yeah, unbelievable," agreed Alice.

"Back to your question. I don't think someone can explain this phenomenon with details and reasoning… yet. However, if you are really interested in scientific explanations, I recommend that you read Rupert Sheldrake's books. He is a UK biologist and made a great observation that we are connected and affect each other through morphogenetic fields. We cannot detect these fields, but we can see or perceive their effect."

"Morpho-what?" Alice asked.

"Morphogenetic fields," repeated Mary slowly with a smile.

"If you look around, you can see that it's not just us, but all people who naturally or historically form social groups for the purpose of survival. It's really hard, even impossible, for someone to survive in the wilderness on their own, especially children and the elderly. We share this world with animals, birds, fish, and insects that also somehow realize that they might live longer if they stay together. It simply creates a safer place, a greater chance for survival."

Alice's imagination immediately started unfolding pictures of a pack of wolves, a school of fish, a flock of birds, and a herd of bulls, and how it helps to survive their offspring and species in general when they belong to their group.

"Thanks to this wise order," Mary continued, "species live for thousands or millions of years. Rupert Sheldrake observed that each group, as a living organism, forms a morphogenetic field within which each member can receive information about everything concerning the group's functioning and survival.

"You and I are also part of nature, and we also live in social groups that form their morphogenetic field. A family or a tribe is a fundamental group supporting humankind's continuing life by caring for each individual member. In return, each group member grants their loyalty and supports the group. In this mutually beneficial cooperation, each of us has a better chance of survival. In other words, we are all connected through this field.

"That's what you experienced today, and this is how I learned that the world around us contains much more than our minds can grasp through our physical sensory organs and logical minds."

With that, Mary glanced at her watch.

"It's time to go back. Are you done with your coffee?"

Alice nodded, then drained her cup and hurriedly stood up – just as a waiter carrying a tray with two hot coffees and cream cakes was about to pass by the table. Alice had jumped up so quickly and unexpectedly that the waiter did not have time to dodge her. The air was filled with the sounds of breaking glass, splashing liquid, women's screams, and then silence. All participants and witnesses froze in their places, but the next moment, the sounds of voices, quick steps, and moving chairs resumed.

Mary and two other waiters surrounded Alice, removing the last of the whipped cream from the bottom of her pale pink blouse. The left side of her light blue jeans was soaked with spilled coffee.

For a moment or two, Alice had felt like she was watching a slow-motion movie in which she was the main character. She felt how fright and burning pain gave way to irritation and anger, then were replaced by feelings of shame, guilt, and resentment.

Alice was so overwhelmed that she couldn't think much and automatically answered questions that she was okay.

Mary also was shocked for a moment. It seemed as though some unknown forces intervened and interrupted their plans.

"I don't understand how it happened," Alice spoke, almost in tears. "What a nightmare." She looked down at the huge wet, greasy stains on her clothes. "I'm sorry, Mary, but I have to go home."

"Yes, of course," Mary answered. "May I call a cab for you?

"That would be great, thanks. I just hope the driver won't object to me sitting on the seat in dirty clothes." She sighed with disappointment. "Tell Sara I am very sorry that I will not be able to participate in the seminar."

"It's okay, Alice. I think for some reason you don't need the second part of Sara's program."

Alice looked at her in surprise.

"Over the years, I have noticed that there are no random people at these energy seminars. Invisible forces sometimes bring people there who did not even plan to attend. And sometimes those forces do not let those who were looking forward to the seminar get to the seminar. At the last moment, something happens unexpectedly. I trust that the Universe knows best what is right for each of us at this moment. Don't be upset. I love you."

"Okay," Alice said as they hugged, although she didn't quite understand, she did trust her friend.

CHAPTER ELEVEN

It was a rainy Saturday afternoon. John had left to visit his parents, the children went to practice, and Alice could finally focus on her upcoming work presentation. The sudden loud ringing of the phone made her flinch.

She answered and was surprised to hear Bella's agitated voice on the other end.

"Alice, hello! Are you busy?"

"Hi, Bella! What's up?"

"Do you have a minute? Can we talk?"

Alice glanced at the pile of papers on her desk and replied, "Yeah, did something happen?"

"I'm pregnant," blurted out Bella. "I don't know what to do!"

For a moment, Alice was stunned speechless.

"Well…" she said, slowly drawing out her words to buy her some time. "It sounds like this isn't exactly happy news…?"

"How can I be happy when my husband is furious about this? He yelled at me. He was so angry at me. I don't know what to do." Bella said again, her voice quivering.

"Wait. Not so fast. Tell me the story," Alice said. A soft sob could be heard on the phone.

"Okay. We were celebrating our son's birthday about two months ago. Fred had a few drinks, and everything was going so well. We hadn't had a close relationship for a long time ... and then all of a sudden ... you know ... everything was so good. Fred hates condoms. It's always been my responsibility to avoid pregnancy. I used vaginal suppositories for contraception. I checked...they were still within their expiration date." Bella moaned. "I don't know how this happened.

"When I found out I was pregnant, I was happy at first. I thought it was such an excellent opportunity to revive our marriage and start all over again…"

"Well, what did Fred say to that?"

"I told you, Alice, he became furious. He insulted me and shouted that I had planned it! He also said that I am brainless…that, at my age, it is time to think about grandkids…not children." Bella sobbed again and fell silent for a second.

"Long story short, Fred wants me to have an abortion. He said he will pay for everything."

Alice had some very clear, very unflattering thoughts about Fred in that moment, but she didn't vocalize them. Instead, she just asked, "So… Fred wants to get rid of his child."

Suddenly she recalled Mary's question about the soul and asked, "And what does Bella want?"

The line went silent then as Alice waited patiently for an answer.

"I want a baby," said Bella finally, and in a such deep voice that it could only be a cry of her heart. "I already love him. When I was young, I did not fully realize all the joys of motherhood. I had many desires and ambitions to achieve something in life. And now everything looks different…much of what was so important before has lost its importance, and what was taken for granted has acquired its significance. My son and family have become my most important thing…

"And you know what, Alice?" she continued, "I always wanted a second child. But something always got in the way – either I needed to finish my studies, or we didn't have enough money, moved to another city, or something else."

"Well, then, have the baby," Alice said simply.

"And how do you imagine I can do that?" Bella asked irritably. She paused. "Fred said he wasn't going to live with me anyway."

Alice didn't have time to process this shocking announcement.

"How can I cope on my own?" Bella sobbed. "How will I support the child? And how will the child grow up without a father?"

"Yes, this is a complicated situation," agreed Alice, and it will not be easy. "But my grandmother used to say that if God gives a child, God will give *for* a child."

"What would you do if you were in my shoes?" Bella asked.

"I wouldn't have married Fred in the first place…" Alice tried to defuse the situation with humor, though of course she wasn't really joking. "But to be honest, I don't know. In a case like this, it's hard to give advice, and it would be best if you did not listen to any. This is a very intimate decision. And I respect and support whatever choice you make."

"Thank you," Bella replied, touched. "Okay, I'll let you go. I'm very grateful to you for this conversation. I needed someone to talk to."

"Please call me anytime if you need anything," Alice said, then hung up the phone with a sigh.

She felt pity for Bella, and resentment on behalf of all the women of the world who faced such a heartbreaking choice. And anger rose in her soul toward men who do not want to take responsibility for their actions and could protect the mother of their child at a time both were most vulnerable.

Then Alice's thoughts turned to her own husband. An image flashed through her mind of John walking around the room for half the night with their first child in his arms when Alice was exhausted. John had always helped take care of their children. With warmth and gratitude in her heart, Alice once again noted what a good husband she had.

Maybe I'm just having a midlife crisis, she thought. *Maybe I just need to overcome it, to come to terms with everything as it is.*

Then she heard another voice reply quietly but with confidence, *This relationship has come to an end. Betraying yourself will not save you or your relationship.*

The sound of the front door opening and the children's voices brought Alice back to the reality of everyday life.

"Ouch! I completely forgot about dinner ..." Alice murmured and hurried to the kitchen.

CHAPTER TWELVE

The red apple of the sun slowly sank into the dark sea waves. Here and there, the stars, small and big, bright and dim, began to light up in the sky. Alice and Mary settled down on loungers close to the water's edge of a deserted beach.

The sounds of music and joyful voices of vacationers came from the dance floor located just behind the strip of slender cypresses that separated the hotel property from the bike path and the golden sandy beach beyond.

Despite the pleasing sounds of rhythmic music, the two friends, tired of the bustle of the city, preferred the mellow sound of the surf. Alice inhaled the air filled with the intoxicating aromas of wisteria and honeysuckle with rapture. The edges of her delicate turquoise chiffon tunic fluttered slightly in the wind, pleasantly caressing her tanned slender legs. Lounging in that chair, Alice was finally allowing herself to relax physically and mentally. It had certainly been the right decision to take a few days off and join Mary in this beautiful place.

From a distance, things seem different, she thought, hoping that this short vacation on neutral territory would also give her the chance to sort out her thoughts and feelings.

The soft light of twinkling stars streamed down to the ground. A bright orange moon rose over the sea, spreading a shivering silvery path on the water. The women watched with awe the uncovering majesty of the infinite Universe, where the brightness of humming day transformed into majestic night. The Universe embraced Alice and Mary lovingly, covering them with its starry shawl.

"So many stars…" whispered Mary reverently. "Look, there is the North Star!" She stretched her hand up, pointing to one of the brightest stars, adding, "It is the only one I recognize.

"As a schoolgirl, I was amazed that there was a mother bear and her cub that always traveled together through the night sky. My teacher told me that if I could find them among billions of other stars, I could spot the North Star and it would show me the way home when I was lost."

That's exactly what I need, thought Alice, *to find my way because I'm lost.*

"Have you ever considered that we, people, also form and belong to our constellations and galaxies by creating our families?"

It was as if Mary was responding to Alice's unspoken statement.

"Do you think so?" she asked, shifting her gaze from the panorama of the night sky to her wise friend.

"Each star born has its specific and meaningful place within its constellation. You and I are also part of our families, countries, and cultures, and each of us has a unique place that belongs to us by birthright." Mary spoke in a calm, melodious voice, as if she were singing. Mesmerized by the sound and the sight above, Alice tilted her head again, peering into infinity.

The bright yellow moon that just moments earlier was so close to the horizon became small and pale as it rose over the women's heads.

"Everything in the Universe is moving," continued Mary. "You and I, like stars, are also in constant motion throughout our lives. This non-stop rotation creates an illusion that planets and stars are changing their locations. However, we can see how the cosmic mother bear and baby bear travel together every night. Isn't it wonderful?" Mary added dreamily.

Alice silently nodded her head in agreement.

"If we can acknowledge and remain at our cosmic place, we may receive strength and support from our ancestors."

"Our cosmic place?" Alice asked in confusion, "What is that?'

"Another difficult question..." said Mary, smiling. "Simply put, it is where we can joyfully shine.

"Again, just like a star in its constellation, you and I have our own place in our family system. Each system has its own structure and obeys certain rules. Bert Hellinger wrote about one hundred books explaining that, but it's better to see or experience once instead of listening to multiple boring explanations. So, ask Sara during her next family constellations workshop. She will show you how to identify and maintain your place in your family or your business."

"Okay…" Alice said slowly, "I'm not sure I understand what you are talking about, but it sounds comforting. Now, please, keep going. Tell me more about the stars and the Universe."

CHAPTER THIRTEEN

Mary pulled out a linen wrap from her bag and threw it over her naked shoulders, sheltering herself from the freshness of the night breeze. She leaned back in her chair and stared thoughtfully at the moon surrounded by billions of dancing stars.

"In my mind, the wisdom of humanity is what was consciously accepted from the wisdom of the Universe," she began.

"The wisdom of nature is the infinite wisdom of God or Creator or any other name you use to name the Great Power behind all creations. The wisdom of nature takes many forms, in diversity and volume. Everything is here in various forms of being, where nothing is taken out of context. Everything is intertwined in the Universe's unbounded manifestations. The visible is connected with the tangible, felt, and invisible, but is experienced as a whole. You and I are parts of this miraculous Universe," Mary paused, deeply inhaling as if she was drinking the air.

"Feel it," she said. "Breathe it in! We all breathe the same air. I inhale what you exhale and vice versa. Air is not just a mixture of gases. It includes particles of light. It is an invisible soup of energy. We connect with each other and everything around us through each breath we take."

Alice's eyebrows rose in surprise. As usual, Mary had introduced an idea that she had never considered before.

Like her other friends and acquaintances, she had been actively involved in the struggle for survival, for a place under the sun, for most of her life. Questions of the Universe had always made her uncomfortable, until something within started sending alarms, telling her that her life had reached the point where the battle for physical survival had come at the cost of her spiritual life.

"In this holographic world," Mary continued, "the entire Universe contains billions of other Universes, and each of them is just a grain of sand within the whole. Nothing exists without being connected to the whole. Everything is permeated with wisdom and love. Everything touches, intertwines, and interacts with everything through the connection of threads of love. Some call it the web of life."

"The pattern of the Universe is woven with threads of love," she repeated. "This pattern can be partially examined through developed, expanded perception as the physical sense organs cannot see and perceive beyond their physical limitations. Our linear minds cannot process what goes beyond cause-and-effect connections. If you are not a physicist, it's hard to accept the ideas of quantum physics. Anyway, believe it or not, everything is vibrating in its creative frequencies."

Alice's imagination drew a picture of a vast woven fabric where destiny's intricate, colorful patterns were threaded through with divine love.

"I love to reflect on the topic of the Universe," Mary said. "But it's hard – I would say impossible – to put such an enormous, complex thing into words." She glanced at Alice. "How can you describe the wind to someone who has never experienced or witnessed this movement of air?

"It is the same with our feelings. Our logical mind divides everything into parts, makes them compacted, and compares them with something already well-known. When everything is broken into parts for the convenience of understanding, the connections are lost or overlooked because it is assumed that the parts are more important than the connections between them."

Alice looked at her then, for she felt the notes of sadness in her friend's voice.

"Imagine for a moment a human body," Mary said. "Each organ is individually essential because it performs a specific function; however, they also must work in concert because if they don't the body, as a system, cannot function."

"To be honest, I don't understand why this matters," said Alice. "The majority of people live without thinking about it."

"You are right; for many, everything we are talking about now is nonsense. And that's fine. We all are evolving." Mary smiled and added, "Every fruit has its time."

"So you are saying that the Universe is a large system within which there are infinite other systems?" Alice asked.

"Absolutely."

"And, as reasonable people," Alice said, "we see only the visible parts of systems, like these randomly scattered stars. If we look carefully and for a long time, we can see some star patterns, but we do not see what holds them together…"

"Exactly! It's the same concept we can apply to a family system. Each family is a powerful network of interconnected destinies, and that is what Sara showed us last time."

"Oh yes, I had an amazing experience," Alice replied, "I still regret missing part of the seminar because of this stupid coffee."

Mary looked at Alice with a wide smile. "Yes, we played with invisible forces, and they played with us."

Alice turned to her friend, then the two of them burst out laughing.

CHAPTER FOURTEEN

Alice and Mary were still chuckling over what they now referred to as "the coffee incident" when their attention was diverted by the sound of people arguing. The loud voices were angry, and they were getting closer.

Sure enough, they saw two dark figures, a man and a woman, hurrying in their direction. More curious than frightened, Alice and Mary stared in their direction, when suddenly a light and shadow spectacle unfolded in front of their eyes.

A beautiful woman's silhouette loomed in the moonlight as if a magical goddess had appeared from the sea. She wore a maxi skirt that wrapped her well-shaped hips and a fitted top with spaghetti straps that accentuated her breasts. Despite her rapid gait, her movements were smooth and graceful.

A moment later, the man appeared on the moonlighted stage. Sometimes he sharply waved his muscular arms as if drawing or pointing something in the air. He spoke emotionally and loudly as if the volume of the sound could help prove his case. The woman mainly listened to him, though from time to time she would loudly respond with a verbal attack of her own. The young couple was so immersed in their grievances that neither of them appeared to notice Alice and Mary, who were staring in rapt attention just a few feet away. They also seemed oblivious to the fragrant night breeze and the silvery surf of gentle waves.

"Stop comparing me with someone else," yelled the man. "I try my best for the family; I work tirelessly. But whatever I do, it never satisfies you! Look, I brought you here so you could rest, it's still not good enough. You're making me crazy!"

He shook his head and ran a strong hand through his dark, wavy hair; his eyes flashed with indignation. Every now and again the breeze would ruffle his unbuttoned shirt, exposing his pumped-up torso.

"Stop yelling at me. Everything I do or say annoys you," the woman retorted.

She said something else, but they were too far at that point for Alice and Mary to make out the words.

"What a beautiful couple…I feel so sorry for them," said Alice as their dark silhouettes melted into the darkness.

"Yeah…They looked like a god and goddess." Mary's voice grew whimsical again. "Do you know that Mars, the god of war, and Venus, the goddess of love and beauty, had a daughter named Harmonia?"

"I had no idea," said Alice, surprised by her friend's abrupt change of subject. "I even didn't know they had a child."

"Actually, they had three children, but the scene we just witnessed made me think of Harmonia."

Somehow this news had a calming effect on Alice. She imagined gentle and loving Venus next to a passionately angry Mars and their beautiful daughter Harmonia.

"Do you think Mars and Venus also had fights?" asked Alice.

"Oh, I'm ninety-nine-point-nine percent sure they did."

Alice chuckled. "Well, I'm glad we didn't witness a conflict between them. I would not want the thunder of battles to disturb our pleasant evening." She paused. "But why are you so sure that they fought?"

"Because as long as we divide everything into light and darkness or right and wrong, we will fight with each other," said Mary slowly, as if weighing each word. "All wars are battles of ideas. This is because there is no common understanding of 'good' and 'evil' in this complex world. Very often, what is suitable for one is bad for another, and vice versa. This one-sided perspective is a major source of any level of conflict."

"Why is that so?" asked Alice.

"I don't know. This is how this world of duality operates. If you look at our lives, each of us has gone through a long training on the proper understanding of good and evil, right and wrong, just and unjust. I like how Don Miguel Ruiz termed it: a process of domestication. So, like everybody else, you and I received a collection of established ideas about everything. This is how our family and community prepared us for life in human society. They granted us their protection and support in exchange for our obedience and loyalty. It helped us to survive."

Mary inhaled deeply and with pleasure. On the exhale, she looked into the distance to where the water's edge merged with the dark sky.

"Have you ever watched the movie *Jonathan Livingston Seagull*?" she asked. "It's based on the book of the same name by Richard Bach."

"I don't think so," said Alice, looking in the distance. "What is it about?"

"It's about society," she replied matter-of-factly. "Anyone who doesn't follow the rules of his flock or has contradictory ideas will be cast out… in the best-case scenario. The worst-case scenario is that if society feels threatened by their freethinking member, they will declare him an enemy and kill him."

A shadow of sadness ran across Mary's face, and she shook her head as if to drive the feeling away.

"It's a beautiful movie…just birds, sea, and music. But it's actually about us… Anyway, back to your question. That handsome, angry man we just saw believes that his ideas about what is right are the most righteous, and his beautiful companion believes that her right is more right than his right. That's funny, right?" Mary laughed.

"They grew up in diverse families and obeyed different rules to guarantee their right to belong. And now, these two worlds of ideas crossed or, more accurately, collided. The question is whether they can give their love a chance and find a balance in their relationship…to give birth to harmony."

"I don't like conflicts," Alice stated firmly. "I always tried to avoid them at any cost."

"I don't think each conflict is necessarily a negative thing," Mary said. "Very often, whether it's an inner or outer conflict, it pushes us toward life-changing decisions. It brings to the surface something that has been suppressed for a long time. In a case like that couple, a conflict may serve to heal a situation where tension and contradictions have bubbled beneath the surface.

"You know what I think?" she asked with a mischievous smile.

Alice nodded her head.

"We should be grateful for people who challenge us. They give us a chance to grow."

Alice didn't know what to say. Her head felt like it was beginning to swell from so many unusual and indigestible ideas.

"So, based on what you said, those people that we believe are bad are actually good, and those whom we think are good are preventing us from the growth – and that is not good." Alice paused. "Interesting."

"Yep! Of course, it depends on the situation. But an outcome of a constructive conflict is an expanded perception of the world," said Mary. "And who knows, maybe this couple will be able to let go of some old limiting ideas and see each other and the world around them differently."

Alice turned her head toward Mary. Even as their eyes met, her friend's words took her somewhere in the world of her memory and imagination. Alice thought about John, Bella, and the young couple.

"Where is the love in all these stories?!" she blurted out before she could stop herself.

Mary looked at her quizzically. "Love …? So many people talk about their love, but can anyone explain the meaning of this word?"

Her eyes sparkled again with joyful mischief. "Many years ago, I read a humorous poem, and I don't know why but it stuck in my head. It went like this:

I love my dog. I love my cat.

I love my husband and his bouquet.

I love my country. I love my car.

I love my parents and credit card.

I love my children. I love my shoe.

Love in the air. I love you too…

"Isn't that funny? Google the meaning of the word love." Mary paused, and when she spoke again her tone had changed from glee to sadness. "Actually, it is not funny. It's ridiculous.

"I believe 'love' is another word that has many meanings. Usually, we use it to describe something that brings pleasure, satisfaction, a sense of belonging, or any other benefits we receive from an object of our love.

For example, one can say, 'I love my dog. I have so much fun with him/her"; or 'I love my country. It protects me and provides different sorts of opportunities for me'; 'I love my garden. It grounds and joys me when I see and smell my roses; 'I love you. I am romantically and sexually attracted to you. I want you. I want to share the rest of my life with you.'

"This love assumes possession of a favorite object or attachment to it," Mary continued. "It's like a swing that lifts us emotionally up to the sky when we are in love and ruthlessly throws us down when the object of love is gone. People describe this love as conditional, as it always has a reason for existence. And I assume your question is not about this sort of love," said Mary. "Because that kind is everywhere."

"You are right… this is not the love I want to experience." Alice smiled. "When I was a teenager, I read a lot of poetry. But I only remember a line or two, certainly not a whole verse.

"What am I looking for? I'm looking for the love that's as divine as a star fall. And if I can't have that…well, I don't need any more of the other kind."

"That's beautiful," said Mary. "It's very poetic and romantic. It creates a feeling of space and sounds as it talks about Universal, unconditional love. Many of us dream of unconditional love. This love accepts everyone as they are, without any expectations; it equally turns its loving flow toward just and unjust.

This love is an excellent gift for those who can open their hearts and minds to give and receive it. This love gives freedom."

She didn't know if it was Mary's words or the sudden chilly breeze, but a chill ran over Alice's skin. It was only now that she noticed that the singing of crickets had replaced the noise of the disco, and the empty dance floor had plunged into the fragrant, thick darkness of the night.

It's getting chilly… time to go to the hotel, she thought.

"It's getting late. Let's go get some rest," Mary said as if reading Alice's mind.

Squinting and fumbling in the darkness, the friends gathered their belongings and headed toward the illuminated path that led to the hotel. The peace and silence of the surrounding space filled Alice's loving heart and spilled forth, just as the divine star fall she had spoken of.

Suddenly, the song *What a Wonderful World* ran through her mind. And, indeed, in that moment, it was.

CHAPTER FIFTEEN

A lice stood on the platform, waiting for the subway train that would take her to the shopping mall. The smell of the railroad tracks irritated the lining of her sensitive nose. She felt how the air was being pushed out of the tunnel by the approaching train. With a loud howl of a siren, the train appeared at the opening of a dark underpass, then colorfully dressed, stony-faced passengers in the cars quickly passed before Alice's eyes.

The train braked noisily and the car door opened right in front of Alice. She stepped forward when suddenly Bella came out, literally colliding with her. For a moment the women froze in amazement at the happy coincidence. As they greeted each other, Alice, who was in no hurry, decided to skip the train so they could chat.

"So happy to see you!"

"Me too!" replied Bella. "How are you? Any exciting news?"

"Everything is fine…Nothing exciting. You know…work, home…same old routine…"

She trailed off, the unspoken question hanging between them. It had been a couple of months since that shocking conversation about the difficult decision Bella was facing.

She certainly looked well. Bella was dressed in a dark cherry fitted coat with a round turned-down collar on which an amber spider spread its thin golden legs. A bright scarf with a geometric pattern that matched the color of her coat was tied to the strap of her shoulder bag.

"What about you?" Alice asked tentatively, "Any exciting news to share?"

Bella understood the hidden question. She looked down, paused, and then looked straight at Alice.

"I had to have an abortion," she said, with tears and a deep sadness welling up in her eyes.

Bella took her bag off her shoulder and started rummaging through it. Alice took her gently by the elbow and pulled her to the side, away from the bustling crowd. Bella finally found a tissue in her bag and dabbed at her eyelashes, careful not to smudge the thick layer of mascara.

"I'm so sorry," Alice said sympathetically, sorry she had asked.

"It's okay," Bella sniffed, "You are the only one I can talk with about that."

Alice kept silent, for she had nothing to say. She also knew Bella needed a space to vent her feelings.

"I tried to convince Fred to keep the child, and when he said no I tried to convince myself that I could care for it on my own. But none of that mattered. The doctor said my kidneys would not withstand the pregnancy and may fail at any moment." Bella sighed and dabbed her eyelashes again.

"I was still hoping for a miracle, but my legs started to swell a lot and I gave up. I killed my baby…my hope. I will never forgive my husband…he betrayed me…he crushed my love," Bella burst into sobs.

 Alice's own eyes filled with tears. She could feel her friend's deep, aching grief and did not know how to console her. How could one console a woman who one moment was a conduit for life and the next felt like an empty shell? Such an emotional trauma would not heal for a very long time, if it did at all.

So she just silently listened to Bella's cry, knowing tears would at least release some of those painful emotions that had been locked up.

"Anyway, Fred and I are back to our everyday life as if nothing happened," said Bella. "I'm trying not to think about that because it's not like I can change it. This is my fate." She looked down at the stained tissue in her hand and exclaimed,

"Oh, my God, my mascara!" then began to rummage through her bag again, this time to retrieve a compact mirror.

"Do you want to go to a cafe and talk?" Alice asked gently.

"Oh no!" Bella hastily replied. "I have many things planned for today." She reached out and squeezed Alice's hand. "But thank you very much. Next time, let's call Nina and July, and have a party. Okay, I have to run."

Then her dark cherry silhouette disappeared into the many-faced motley crowd.

Alice stood there for a few more minutes, looking into the space that had just swallowed Bella and thinking about women's destinies – so similar and so different. The sound of an approaching train brought Alice out of her daze and reminded her that she too had somewhere to be.

CHAPTER SIXTEEN

It was another hot Saturday evening when Alice went outside to water plants exhausted by the scorching sun. A light breeze cooled down the hot air, and the fresh water combined with grass and soil filled the air with a delightful aroma. Alice was gazing at the sky where planets and stars were like little bulbs, one by one, turned on by an invisible hand. Alice said hi to Venus, her usual evening companion, and focused on various starry sky patterns. She recalled reading somewhere that people were brought to Earth from a distant planet.

Alice was looking at the stars and thinking of that special one that was probably her very first home. She was thinking about a star that, according to her favorite song, lit up her life in this physical world and would remain with her even after her transition.

It's so comforting, she mused, *to know that one of those twinkling stars is showering each of us with love and acceptance even though it is so far away.*

Suddenly she noticed that a tiny shiny star was slowly approaching her. She rubbed her eyes as if to erase an optical illusion, then looked around. It still was there! Alice had never seen something like that. She stood there, mesmerized by the minuscule spark of light flying in front of her. It made several circles and slowly disappeared into the darkness.

"What was that?" Alice asked aloud, her rational mind immediately beginning a process of recognizing and analyzing.

This is a sign, her heart replied immediately with a loud pounding in her chest.

Alice agreed. Almost a year had passed since she shared with Mary her desire to divorce John. But she still couldn't bring herself to admit to John that their relationship had come to an end. She kept waiting for some miracle... a sign from the Universe. This was it.

She would talk to John tonight. Yes the question remained, what was that tiny flying spark?"

The next moment, she got a reasonable answer. It was nothing more than a firefly that, as a tiny star, floated past her. But it didn't matter; to Alice that bug had delivered guidance from the Universe.

Alice recalled Mary's words: "The Universe is talking to us through everything that surrounds us – stars, planets, crystals, animals, people, magical creatures, and so on. Unfortunately, we are often too busy to pause and listen, to feel the vast greatness to which each of us belongs. Each of us has access to its wisdom. This understanding comes from experience. To get experience, first, one has to choose to become a seeker."

"I'm ready…I can do it," Alice encouraged herself.

She turned off the water, took a deep breath, and with a confident step, walked toward the glass sliding door from which a warm light streamed, illuminating her path.

Alice resolutely entered the house, ignoring the familiar shadow of doubt, and called out to her husband.

A moment later, John appeared in the kitchen doorway.

"What's the matter?"

"I need to tell you something," replied Alice.

"All right, I'm listening." He sat down on a wooden chair with carved arms near the table and gave her his full attention. Alice thought she saw an anxious look cross his face, but nevertheless began the fateful speech she had rehearsed so many times in her mind.

"John, we have lived so many years together, and I am truly grateful for all you have done and continue to do for the children and me…"

John didn't say anything, but she could tell he didn't like the start of the conversation.

"The fact is that everything in our lives has changed, and I feel that I need to be alone and figure out how to live the rest of my life."

She spoke the words quickly, as if that would soften the blow of what was happening.

John furrowed his eyebrows, staring at the flowery tablecloth on the table as if trying to understand his wife's words. He looked at Alice briefly and then at the floor. She could almost sense what he was thinking, that despite her earlier hints of her unhappiness it never truly occurred to him that one day she might leave.

For a few minutes, there was complete silence in the kitchen, broken only by the occasional rumbling of the refrigerator. It was for both of them a total collapse of their world, though much more for John who looked as though he had been struck by lightning. Alice did not dare look at him; if she did, her guilt might cause her to take back a decision that she had already put off for far too long.

"I'm thinking of renting an apartment so we can live apart," said Alice, carefully sidestepping the word divorce.

John, looking somehow smaller and wilted, was quiet for a moment, then he said, "You don't need to go anywhere. I'll move in temporarily with my parents, and then we'll see."

Alice felt deep sadness and, at the same time, relief. Finally, she had told the truth, and she had set herself free. Thank God, she told herself, the conversation had gone much more smoothly than she thought.

It would take a decade and much more study of Universal love before Alice realized how much love John had shown her by letting her go without drama. Yet not once in those ten years had she regretted her decision. Despite the painful breakup, she knew that both of them had opened a new chapter in their lives that would bring joyful and meaningful experiences. She also knew that the threads of love that had brought them together in this life would remain forever. John would later tell her about that when he appeared in one of Alice's vivid dreams.

He was looking at her, his gaze was foggy, and Alice asked him, "John, can you see me?"

"I cannot see you…" he replied, "but I feel you… I can feel you anywhere and anytime despite the distance between us in space or time. We are connected forever by limitless love. Our love is bigger than us."

EPILOGUE

The rhythmic sound of hooves breaks the morning silence. The round-faced moon, lingering after a night walk, is watching with interest the silhouette of a horse carrying a rider that appears against the background of the rising sun.

A bay horse rushes along the seashore's edge, with Alice, flushed from the fresh air, on its back. Splashes of water sparkling in the sun fly from under the horse's hooves. The wide sleeves of Alice's snow-white tunic flutter in the wind like the wings of a white-winged gull against the background of the azure sea.

"Hello, Sun!" Alice joyfully greets the rising fiery orb and playfully winks at the Moon, saying to her, "I am surprised to see you at this time. But I am glad you are here."

After an hour of riding, Alice has the sense that she and her long-maned horse Fate can communicate telepathically. Fate had carried Alice with care and confidence. Alice bends down to the horse and quietly whispers, "Thank you, dear! It looks like we can speak to each other without words."

She stops the horse, then straightens up and looks into the distance as if trying to spot someone. "I wouldn't be surprised," she adds joyfully, "if Neptune appeared here now. Someone told me that Neptune provides us with intuition and inspiration. Look at this divine view. I wish I was an artist...I would paint it."

The horse periodically snorts excitedly, as if he truly comprehends and agrees with all she is saying.

Alice is close to the truth. Her celestial friends have been nearby all the time.

Bright sunlight made them invisible; nevertheless, Alice recognizes their presence. Alice is grateful to Mars for the confidence and courage to move on with life. She appreciates the energy of transformation she receives from Pluto. She had needed that energy badly during the last several years to accept herself and her life the way it was. A stream of feminine power had flowed from Venus, empowering and assisting her.

"Hooray! Alice has become a star that radiates her authentic light!" shouted Uranus in celebration of her uniqueness.

Alice feels a little dizzy from overflowing energy. The world has ceased to be alien and hostile. Rather, on the contrary, she has become a unique part of this diverse world.

Mary was so right about the feeling of being alone, she thinks. *Now I can see and feel that I am never completely alone in this world.*

Alice opens her arms as if she wants to embrace the whole world. She breathes in unison with the majestic humming ocean, swaying fragrant herbs, a couple of soaring eagles, and non-stop working ants.

She feels whole and complete. She accepts her past with everything that belonged to it and is fully aware that she is in charge of her life. She recognizes her strengths and weaknesses and knows that her immature and frightened inner child still needs her help to become an adult.

She can see how much life energy she spent trying to understand why almost no one saw her for who she was. Finally, she saw the truth: that most of the people she had met in her life saw themselves as reflected by her. It might be helpful to create and support an idea about oneself to survive in the world of duality, however, to discover the true self one didn't need an intermediary. One needed only the courage to face their traumatized and frightened inner child and bear the responsibility to help this immature part of themselves become an adult.

"My dear inner child," she said. "Let me hug you with all my heart. Feel how the light of love connects us by an invisible thread. The same strings of love connect us with other people who are present or were present in our life, who stood at the origins of our family, and who will come to our family later. You and I are part of this luminous web woven from the light of love. At this very moment, you and I are in the service of life.

"We combine many immense worlds, both spiritual and physical, in the past and in the future. We also each have our own unique place in this world. Don't be scared anymore, for I will take care of you. I will protect you. I will show you this world full of illusions. You will see that conditional love is inevitable, at least for the foreseeable future, just because it is convenient and often helps to survive in this dual world. But there is another kind of love …one that treats us equally as a sun that shines a light on everyone without dividing them into good and evil. And there is no darkness. It's just a shadow created by natural or artificial objects.

"Our mind is an excellent shadow-maker. Our heart is a generator of light of love that dissolves mind-created barriers and serves the divine wholeness of the Universe."

Alice hugs her horse tighter. She feels pleasure from how, with every breath, every cell of her body is saturated with the aromas of herbs and the sea.

"I am alive! I can feel! Here it is – happiness, the freedom to be myself."

Alice pulled lightly on the reins, and Fate slowly moved forward along the path leading to the next stage in life.

She is ready for a new day, for new challenges. She knows the Great Power will not put more than she can handle on her shoulders. She also knows the Universe is always watching, supporting, and protecting her. She believes that the Guardian Angels that brought her onto the Earth will lead her through this life and take her back to whence she came when it is time.

She is loved. She belongs. She is enough.

ABOUT THE AUTHOR

Viktoria was born and grew up in Soviet Ukraine. Her father was a construction worker, and her mother was an opera singer.

In her native Kyiv, she earned master's degrees in Economics and Information Control Systems and Technologies and built a career, going from a baker to a banker and a general manager of an outsourcing office.

Also in Kyiv, Viktoria met her first husband and gave birth to her three children. She traveled far and often, to the Czech Republic, the UK, Turkey, Poland, Estonia, Austria, Russia, and Greece; however, it was a trip to India at the beginning of 2000 that dramatically changed her life. She divorced, quit her job, moved to the US with her two youngest kids, and started all over.

Through it all, Viktoria believed that some invisible forces were leading her to the right places at the right times. After arriving in the States, she learned English and started teaching economics at a local college. Viktoria's English tutor brought her to the Unity church, where she joined the chorus and met the man who is now her husband.

Viktoria was introduced to the Family Constellation work and dreamt of studying from Bert Hellinger years before she immigrated. The Universe opened this opportunity for her in 2013. For several years Viktoria traveled back and forth to Germany and Mexico to attend the Hellinger School's experiential seminars, eventually becoming a certified Family Constellations facilitator.

The insights and expanded perception she developed during the training became helpful in her teaching profession. Several times, her students nominated her for "Favorite Teacher of the Year."

Viktoria offers online sessions and Family Constellations workshops in Texas and Ukraine. She is committed to helping people create a positive sense of self, meaningful relationships, and a healthy balance in their personal and work lives.

Viktoria has enjoyed gardening since childhood, and one of the first things she did after arriving in the US was to plant an orange tree. Gardening since has become her favorite hobby, and nature her wise teacher, constantly showing how the visible is connected to the invisible.

Viktoria lives in and works from the Gulf Coast of Texas.

Visit her at www.viktoriapierce.com.

LET YOUR STAR SHINE!

Thank you for reading my book. It has been a privilege to share Alice's journey of self-exploration and empowerment with you. I love exploring the hidden forces affecting our personal and professional lives.

If you would like to continue this journey with me in search of inner harmony, forgiveness, and reconciliation through expended perception and spiritual growth, below are ways I may assist you.

- Take my **Universal Orders** class. This online class is a welcoming, safe, and inclusive place where you can explore the world of invisible connections through meditation and group exercises.

- Visit **viktoriapierce.com** to schedule a one-on-one session.

- Follow my **Family Constellations Center** Facebook page for the Family Constellations workshop and the Universal Orders class schedule:
  facebook.com/pierce.familyconstellations

- Watch my **Youtube Channel** to learn more about Family Constellations and Family Constellators:
  youtube.com/@viktoriapierce4690/videos